The LAST TRAIN

Gordon Titcomb   Paintings by Wendell Minor

A NEAL PORTER BOOK

ROARING BROOK PRESS

NEW YORK

The Last Train *is dedicated with love*
to my daughter, Bevin Titcomb, my son, Nolan Titcomb,
and to the memory of
Gordon & Wendell's dear friend Barbara Capuano. —*G.T.*

For Barb, who helped make this book possible,
and in memory of my mother,
who took me to the depot to see the trains. —*W.M.*

"The Last Train" is a perfect song that captures the imagination of anyone who has stood along the railroad tracks in some little American town. The memories of times past are etched through generations, fading like an old photograph. Gordon Titcomb brings them back together, connecting all their stories in a few short verses that capture, like a time capsule, a way of life few can remember. What a gorgeous tribute this is that preserves as it distills for future generations the life of a little railroad station.

—Arlo Guthrie

There's a little railroad station in the center of our town,
The windows boarded up, the roof is falling down.

If you close your eyes and listen,
you can almost hear the sound
Of those big iron horses
rolling into town.

My Granddad was a railroad man,
  he drove the trains around,
My Daddy, he sold tickets
  till they closed the station down.

Now the tracks that shone like silver, have turned to rusty brown.
Thirty years ago the last train rolled through town.

I'm riding on the
    City of New Orleans,
Thinking 'bout the
    Wabash Cannonball.

Oooooh . . . Midnight Flyer,

Hear that lonesome freight train whistle call.

Old cigar box filled with memories,
my boyhood souvenirs,

The watch they gave my Daddy
when he'd put in twenty years.

Now the flattened copper pennies look like little metal tears
That a railroad cries before it disappears.

A ticket punch that clicked
a million snowflakes every year,

The faded union dues card
of a railroad engineer.

WORKING CARD
Division No. 1004
Located at AURORA, ILL.
W. G. Minor B. of L. E.
Dues $4.00 for Month of JANUARY, 1964
Spec'l $ ___
Assm't $1.00 Fin. Sec'y

I AM A MEMBER
OF THE
B. OF L. E.
AND
I PAY MY WAY

CHESAPEAKE AND OHIO LINES

Each item marks a chapter
in a story we hold dear,
Sweet memories of
a railroad man's career.

Oh, the brakeman
with his oil can,

the porter dressed in white,

The fireman with his shovel full of jet-black anthracite,

Gone now, like a dream
    that slowly faded in the night,
Are the faces of
    this once familiar sight.

Oh, the steam gave way to diesel,
and electric-powered trains.
Now the rails look up at contrails
from jet-powered airplanes.

A blast of steam,
    the whistle screamed its mournful last refrains,
Long silent, though its echo still remains.

AUTHOR'S NOTE

As a young boy, I would often accompany my parents to the local railroad station to await the arrival of a family member or guest that was coming to visit us. The station itself was (and once again is, thanks to the efforts of those who have restored and cared for it), very much like the one that Wendell has so wonderfully painted for you in this book. Another of my early memories is that of spending summer nights at my grandparents' farm and hearing a train whistle off in the distance as I was lying in bed before going to sleep. When I was six years old, my Grandmother took me on a vacation that involved crossing a huge expanse of Canada via railroad. It is funny how some details that I remember from that trip might seem so insignificant, yet they have left indelible memories. Things like the funny-looking key that the porter would use to lower our bunks from their daytime positions, the steaming, porcelain bowls of oatmeal, and small, silver-plated pitchers of cocoa, proudly emblazoned with the railroad company's logo. Or the smell of hot grease that you would encounter as you crossed from one car to another. All of these memories are like a vivid collage of sights, sounds, smells, and emotions that remain forever clear in my mind. As much as the artifacts of the railroad left their impression on me, the people of the railroad left an even greater one. While I never knew the conductors', engineers', or porters' names, I certainly came to know their cheerful smiles and kind ways.

What child did not love singing "I've Been Working on the Railroad"? For me, other railroad songs would follow, like "The Wabash Cannonball." In the early 1970s the Eagles and the Osborne Brothers sang "Midnight Flyer," and my good friend, Arlo Guthrie, recorded Steve Goodman's brilliant, quintessential railroad song, "City of New Orleans." I suspect all of these songs, and many others (my own included), were inspired by the very same thing: the hauntingly melancholy strain of a locomotive's whistle, the rhythmic clack of wheels to rails, but most of all, knowing that the latticework of rails you were looking at or riding on were connected to almost any other place in the country that you could imagine. Steve Goodman recognized that when he penned the brilliant lyric "Ride their father's magic carpet made of steel." This book, and the song that spawned it, were born of the same sentiments.

—Gordon Titcomb

Visit these great RAILROAD MUSEUM web sites:

Railroad Museum of Pennsylvania   www.rrmuseumpa.org
National Railroad Museum   www.nationalrrmuseum.org
Illinois Railway Museum   www.irm.org
Baltimore & Ohio Railroad Museum   www.borail.org
The Union Pacific Railroad Museum   www.uprr.com/aboutup/history/museum
Orange Empire Railway Museum   www.oerm.org
Train Mountain Railroad Museum   www.trainmountain.org
Colorado Railroad Museum   www.crrm.org
Southeastern Railway Museum   www.srmduluth.org
An extensive list of railroad museums can also be found at: www.railmuseums.com/namerica
and at: www.american-rails.com/railroad-museums.html

To hear Gordon Titcomb's recording of "The Last Train" visit www.lasttrainsong.com
A book and audio version of "The Last Train" is available at www.liveoakmedia.com

Text copyright © 2010 Gordon Titcomb
Illustrations copyright © 2010 by Wendell Minor
A Neal Porter Book
Published by Roaring Brook Press
Roaring Brook Press is a division of Holtzbrinck Publishing Holdings Limited Partnership
175 Fifth Avenue, New York, New York 10010
www.roaringbrookpress.com

Distributed in Canada by H. B. Fenn and Company Ltd.

Cataloging-in-Publication Data is on file at the Library of Congress.
ISBN: 978-1-59643-164-5

Roaring Brook Press books are available for special promotions and premiums.
For details contact: Director of Special Markets, Holtzbrinck Publishers.

First Edition November 2010
Printed in November 2010 in the United States of America by Phoenix Color Corp. d/b/a Lehigh Phoenix, Rockaway, New Jersey

3   5   7   9   8   6   4   2